T0300631

Book design: Sandra Rosales
Published: Gold Line Press
http://goldlinepress.com
Gold Line titles are distributed by Small Press Distributions
This title is also available for purchase directly from the publisher
www.spdbooks.org: 800.869.7553

Library of Congress Cataloging-in-Publication Data
Bridge of Knots
Library of Congress Control Number 2022947900
Shue, CE
ISBN 978-1-938900-46-4

CE SHUE

BRIDGE

OF

KNOTS

GOLD LINE PRESS

For Denise, my favorite sister.

1   For a while it was quiet, but the world is starting up again. Restaurants are serving meals inside, music festivals have announced their lineups. Students are attending classes in person again and companies are calling their employees back to formerly empty offices.

People are flying to Hawaii in droves.

I can hear the honking of impatient drivers once more, on their way to very very important places. Bicycles ring their bells as they pass joggers running in the road.

Still, no giant tech buses rumble the street in front of our house, not like they used to. And certain city blocks have been closed to traffic permanently, turning them into pedestrian thoroughfares. Kids ride their scooters down the center of the lane, parents push babies in strollers on the blacktop. Dogs zigzag from one side to the other, following their noses from smell to smell.

The Department of Public Works has erected signs at the end of each intersection stating:

Road Closed
To Through Traffic

2   In our backyard, I can still hear the birds in the oak tree next door—the sparrows' trills, the crows' rowdy cries, the blue jays' tap-tapping as they peck on acorns and drop the hulls to the ground.

I can hear the reverberating buzz of bees.
When one dog barks, all the dogs bark.

And the sirens.
I can hear sirens racing all over the city.
In our neighborhood and beyond.

3   From my first apartment in the city, I could see the spire of a church cathedral through my bedroom window. I would lie awake at night and look at the spire, thinking, *I am here. I am really here.* It seemed hard to believe back then.

I had moved away from the small town where I grew up and come to my soul's home.

The church was on the campus of a Jesuit college several blocks away, and through the window I could just see the tip of the spire, where the bells were housed, lit up against the dark sky. Just that little bit of view was enough.

Years later, I would go to that school, which I had not even known existed before I moved to the city.

And I would study poetry.

My teachers were the last of the Language Poets and I loved them. My favorite teacher walked with a cane and spoke haltingly. He had suffered a stroke many years before. In class, he would set up a boom box and play music by Segovia and Muddy Waters. Later, my father would have a stroke as well, paralyzing the left side of his body.

He would never walk again. He would never speak again.

I learned poetry—its silences, and its cadences—from watching the way my teacher walked with his cane. The way he spoke to me after my father had his stroke.

4   Coyotes have been seen roaming the Marina Green. Two, in particular, a male and a female, come out at dusk and play on Crissy Field.

I watch videos of the handsome couple frolicking in the grass, their fur coats thick and full, and I marvel at the resiliency of nature—how that which was hidden can now be seen.

When my son was four years old, he came to me one day, his brown eyes wide with panic.

"What is it?" I asked, feeling his fear reach across the space between us to take hold of my chest.

"I put a bead in my nose and I can't get it out!" he cried.

I looked into his tiny nostril and there it was, a green plastic bead, lodged far into his nasal passage.

I made him blow while I closed off the unobstructed nostril with my thumb. The green bead tumbled into a waiting tissue.

"Why did you put a bead in your nose?" I asked my son later, after the crying.

"To see if I could," he answered, simply.

An octopus has three hearts and nine brains, and his skin changes colors when he dreams. Each of the octopus's arms has its own brain and can make decisions independently from the others.

5   An old boyfriend once asked me, "Do you think the ends justify the means?"

And I said, "There are no ends. There are only means."

"Ah," he said. "I believe the ends *do* justify the means."

And that's why we broke up, in the end.

We are becoming increasingly virtual, as in *almost*.

Virtual Reality.

Almost Real.

Almost.

This is why I think people love snow so much: It makes the world look new again, a freshly washed blanket.

At night I listen to my husband snore and I imagine the sound is coming from waves rolling onto the beach.

6   Deer kill 200 people every year in the United States. That is more than the fatal attacks by bears, sharks, mountain lions, and alligators combined.

At first the stores ran out of toilet paper and bleach. Then they ran out of bread and water. Then flour and yeast, and so on down the supply chain. For a while we had to line up outside the grocery store wearing our masks. Now we don't have to wait in line anymore, but we're still wearing our masks.

I didn't hoard toilet paper, but I did stockpile antidepressants in case there was a rush at the pharmacies.

"If we really want to survive, we'll start eating bugs," says the bespectacled entomologist on tv. "Insects are plentiful, high in protein and they taste like nuts."

Looking at the man's face, ruddy from years of outdoor bug hunting, I wonder if insects taste like nuts the way rattlesnake is supposed to taste like chicken.

There is an island in the Indian Ocean so remote that the inhabitants try to kill anyone who attempts to land on their beaches. The men stand on the sand with spears, ready to attack those unwise enough to approach. It is illegal for boats to get within three miles of the island's shores.

The world has become a global village, I think as I read about the Andaman Islands, interconnected at the speed of electrons. The islanders have no idea that a pandemic is ravaging the rest of the world; isolation has kept them safe from disease, their traditional way of life still intact.

I, on the other hand, keep trying to leave my life behind, but it keeps turning up anyway, like a bad penny.

7   This story begins, like all stories, with the fairy dust of the
dead.

When my daughter was little, her favorite book was *Goodnight
Moon*. She wanted me to read it to her over and over. Again and again,
the moon. The brush. The old lady saying 'hush.'
At first I didn't understand why. It was so *boring*. I could
barely stay awake myself while I was reading it to her.
Then suddenly, I understood. She *wanted* to be bored—so she
could sleep.
Repetition and rhythm meant safety.
Repetition. Rhythm. Safety.

I wonder what it would feel like to feel real, the way animals
feel real, and interact with the world as real. The great white shark is
always a shark, the grizzly bear is always a bear. Although sometimes
fish pretend to be other kinds of fish, or rocks—they still know they are
pretending.
I don't always know when I'm pretending. I feel virtually real,
even when I'm not being real at all.

When I was in the 3rd grade, my teacher read us a story about
a stuffed rabbit that was so loved that he became a real rabbit. "Why
do you have to wait?" I asked my teacher after the other kids had gone
home. "Why do you have to wait until somebody else loves you, to be

real?"

"It's just a story, dear," my teacher replied. "Don't you think it's a beautiful story?"

I didn't, even though it made me cry. Instead, I thought:
What if nobody ever loves you enough for you to become real?
And: *What if they love you, but what they love isn't the real you?*

What happens then?

Here is a writing prompt: Pick a poem that you would never write yourself, and replace every word in it with a word that has the same number of syllables. After you are finished, walk around in the new poem like a jacket made of words.

8   Marilyn Monroe looked like one thing, and people loved her for it.

But inside she wanted to be something else.

The pandemic is also an epidemic. All pandemics are epidemics, but not all epidemics are pandemics.

Is the earth trying to balance the scales once again?

All this tragedy, to force us to become healthy.

Will the virus kill some of us, so we won't kill all of us?

The cuttlefish's skin changes colors, hypnotizing its prey to be eaten, eaten without knowing what is happening.

By then it's too late.

9   Every artist knows that it is easier to paint when the light is good.

Monet set up several canvases in the field to paint haystacks and moved quickly from one painting to another as the light moved across the sky.

To catch the light, the shadows.

But it's easier to write when it's dark outside.

Emily Dickinson wrote her poems in the middle of the night, when the rest of her family was asleep.

Proust wrote nary a word sitting at a desk; he wrote lying down in his big brass bed.

Because memories are like dreams and dreams are most vivid on the edge of sleep.

And sleep is a whack on the side of the head.

When Odysseus went to fight the Trojan War, his wife Penelope warded off her would-be suitors by continually knitting and unknitting a burial shroud for her father-in-law, Laertes.

The ruse worked for three years.

Because knitting takes as long as fuck.
Anyone who knits knows that.

What if life was a collection of beautiful knots that held itself
together?

10   Sometimes I'll be in in a group of people, talking about things we've heard and seen and I'll think: *Is this how it's done?*

As if personality is chemical.

As if I'm a set of qualities interacting with other sets of qualities.

Then I see my dog napping, twitching as she dreams, and the tension holding me together melts and I am undone.

This is my one super power: I not only know what actor someone's trying to think of, but I know which actor they are confusing with *that* actor. For instance, the actor in *Rogue One* in the *Star Wars* series is Felicity Jones, but they are thinking of Keri Russell, who played a spy in television show *The Americans*. And the woman who plays the villain in *X-Men: Dark Phoenix* is Jessica Chastain, not Bryce Dallas Howard, who was in the fourth *Jurassic Park* movie, the one with Chris Pratt. And the actor with the bad haircut in *No Country for Old Men* is Javier Bardem, not Jeffrey Dean Morgan, who played Mary-Louise Parker's boyfriend in the tv comedy *Weeds*.

Plus: Tilda Swinton and Tom Hiddleston, who played married vampires in *Only Lovers Left Alive*, and Jesse Eisenberg and Mia Wasikowska who made a movie titled, coincidentally, *The Double*. It's not that they get mistaken for one another, but they look like each other, only in the opposite gender.

It is a small super power, but entertaining.

I'm also very good at arriving places before a line forms. This makes me handy to have when going to restaurants, or ice cream shops, or the post office, especially during the holiday season.

11 When my mother called with the news that Dad was in the hospital, she didn't say, "Please come home. We need you." Instead, she sighed and said, "Well, do what you want. I don't know how long your father will be in the ICU."

But I heard her loud and clear.

I booked my flight that night and was at the hospital the next morning.

12   One day I saw a man lying face down on the sidewalk. I stopped my car to see if he was ok.

"Do you want guns?" he asked me, jumping up suddenly. He was well over six feet tall, a fact that I hadn't registered when he was flat on the ground.

"I'll be going now," I replied, edging back towards my car.

"Guns!" the man repeated, vehemently. "Do you want them? Do you have them?"

"Is he all right?" my daughter asked from the passenger seat as I hastily got in and locked the doors.

I gave the man's description, (tall, dark curly hair, wearing black basketball shorts and a white t-shirt) and location to the 911 operator. The woman on the phone sounded weary but promised to send someone to check as soon as she could.

Then my daughter and I continued on our way to the grocery store.

13   As a child, the story I hated the most was *Pinocchio.* I hated Jiminy Cricket. I didn't even like his little waistcoat, his little top hat, and I loved miniature things as a kid.

I didn't think Pinocchio needed a talking bug to tell him what was right and what was wrong, and I hated how Jiminy was always so eager to scold him over every little thing. It seemed especially mean to have Pinocchio's nose grow when he lied—his guilt on display for everyone to see and judge. It was torture waiting for the Blue Fairy to turn him into a real boy. I felt his shame so keenly.

What Pinocchio needed was a therapist, not a conscience. A very small therapist, to help him navigate a world he didn't understand, a world that was not made for him. A tiny Carl Jung, perhaps, or a wee D.W. Winnicott, a pocket-sized Alice Miller, to make sure Pinocchio grew not into Geppetto's child, but into his own person.

There are yoga classes where goats will jump on you when you are in Down Dog, lie by your side when you are in Savasana. They call it Goga.

The baby goats are so adorable, you forget that you are exercising. Even if you don't do any of the poses, you still get the endorphin rush from playing with the animals.

14   After the pandemic began, I started seeing my therapist on Zoom, which I think has improved our relationship. I have always liked talking to her, but I like lying on my own couch while I'm doing it better.

At night when I can't sleep, I watch videos of people doing things like cutting someone's hair or giving someone a scalp massage. There are videos of people applying makeup, others of people stroking microphones with brushes and q-tips and feathers. People post videos of themselves shaving bars of soap into thick slices with pocket knives, others squish foam between their fingers and pop the air pockets on sheets of bubble wrap.

Some talk to their unseen audiences in voices barely above a whisper.

I find the sound of the snipping scissors, the popping bubbles, the cooing voices, soothing; they put me right to sleep.

In my dreams I am everyone's mother, even the devil's. I dream that I am trying to get Satan to brush his teeth because they are covered in black soot, and that is why his smile is so ghastly.

Some people see trouble and run the other way.

My mother is afraid of the water because she never learned how to swim. She watched my father swim every day, however, and that was enough exercise for her.

But when you put your face into the ocean, you see how your straw ends up in the turtle's mouth.

The plastic bag that looks like a jelly fish floating in the sea.

15   They say that if a tree falls in the forest and there is no one there to hear it, it makes no sound.

But there are other trees in the forest, and animals, and insects.

They hear the tree fall.

There was a newspaper article that told the story of a photographer who was swimming in the ocean, taking pictures of sharks feeding on a school of mackerel when suddenly the sky went dark. A sperm whale had scooped him up and he was trapped in the mammal's mouth.

The man said he held his breath, just in case the whale dove into deeper waters.

After a moment, the whale spit the man out, his throat being too small to swallow a human.

So I don't have to worry about that anymore.

16   Three years after my parents were married, before my sister and I were born, my father bought a rundown farm in a town where he didn't know anybody. He added a slanted tile roof to the barn and painted the name "Shanghai Pastures" in red chop suey lettering across the front. Then he started milking cows twice a day every day, seven days a week.

The locals were not impressed.

"That boy is going to go under before the year is out," the old timers said to each other, shaking their heads at my father's folly.

He had bought 200 brown and white Guernsey cows instead of the ubiquitous black and white Holsteins that the other farmers raised. Holsteins were traditionally popular because they produced more milk; my father's Guernseys produced less in volume, but the milk was far richer and yielded more cream. This proved to be a smart business move.

After a time, the dairymen who had scoffed at my father started coming by Shanghai Pastures. "Hey, Chino!" they greeted him. "What do you think about the new grain they're selling at the Feed Store?"

My father, who was not one to hold a grudge, shared his knowledge freely, and in turn, became part of the local business community.

The dairymen may have called him "The Chinaman," but my dad's friends called him "El Jefe," (Spanish for "The Boss"). My sister and I called him "The Chinese Charles Bronson," after the tough-guy actor who chased down bad guys in movies with titles like *Violent City*, *The Stone Killer*, and *Death Wish 4*. He was our family's provider and protector. I wanted to be just like him.

17   Some people wear their masks all the time; others only when they pass by other people.

Some people don't wear masks at all and become angry if someone points it out to them.

I wear my mask, but I try to do it in a way that isn't a rebuke to the people around me. It's all in the eyes, the part of the face people can still see.

My husband and I got our Covid-19 shots as soon as we could find appointments. We had to drive across the Bay Bridge to Oakland, where we wound through the parking lot of the football stadium like viewers at a very popular drive-in movie. Members of the National Guard wearing desert camouflage directed traffic. No one got lost or cut the line; the young men and women of the Guard were cheerfully efficient, happy that nobody was yelling at them or resisting their instructions.

18   The next day I went to an apothecary on Haight Street, though I had never bought herbs before. Arrayed on the wall, they looked like the materials I sometimes used to make paper: yellow petals, small magenta buds, needles like bits of straw.

"Damiana is awesome," the girl behind the counter said. She wore a ring that was attached to a chain that became a bracelet that was shaped like a vine that ended in a flower on her index finger. "Damiana is one of the first herbs I ever interacted with."

I bought the Damiana. And the Blue Lotus, on her recommendation, ritual strength.

I asked her to write down instructions on how to brew the tea, how long to steep the blossoms. She tore a sheet out of a lined notebook and, in looping script, wrote down the information.

"Why don't you print the instructions on the package?" I asked, feeling bad for making the young woman do extra work.

"The FDA won't let us," she replied. "There's some rule about it, something about what's a drug and what's not a drug."

I wondered what ritual I was supposed to know for the Blue Lotus, but was too shy to ask.

"If we print instructions on the package, then it's a drug, or a food, or something," the young woman said. "And if it's a drug or a food, the FDA has to regulate it."

I thanked her for her help and left with my bag of not food/not drugs.

19   I have not loved that many men, a fact that seems embarrassing to me. Related to the Blue Lotus question, in that I cannot ask for certain things.

And after a moment the wanting passes.

There is also the question posed by the Marshmallow Experiment. The principal of my son's elementary school told the anecdote every year on Back to School Night—how children in an educational experiment were asked to choose between eating one marshmallow immediately or receiving two marshmallows if they waited an unspecified amount of time. And how the children who waited for the extra marshmallows became more successful adults than the ones who didn't. Or couldn't.

But what of the children who waited, but wouldn't eat the marshmallows even after they'd been given two? I would wonder each year.

What happened to them?

I'm hoping that the herbs will awaken something in me, something that must still be in seed form, buried deep down inside. A seed that didn't get watered, perhaps, or never felt the warmth of the sun.

This is what I learned in Bali: Never ask the price of an item in the marketplace, unless you want to buy it. Once you engage in a negotiation, you are bound by good faith to pay the best price the two of you come to.

Otherwise, you have wasted the shopkeeper's time, which is rude.

Also, geckoes will poop on you at night because they sleep in the rafters over your bed.

20   I often see something fluttering in the periphery of my vision—a moth? Or is it something else?

If I can dream about a place that I have never been—a city submerged under water, a house floating a foot off the ground, a ship where all the toilets are broken—then dogs must be able to dream about living other lives too, ones with other humans, or maybe no humans at all.

Maybe they dream about driving their own cars.

21 When Mom found my father lying on the den floor, she did what she always did when something surprised or frightened her.

She yelled.

"What are you doing, Royal!?! Get up!"

Only after my father didn't move, did she rush over and ask, "Are you hurt?"

Daddy looked at her and said, "No!"

"Aiya!" she complained, waving him toward a nearby sofa. "Go sit over there!"

We would never know which came first, the stroke or the fall. It could have been either. They lived in a two-story faux Tudor house that was built in the 1980s and had, in the fashion of the times, a step that went up to the kitchen and one down to the living room, as well as another to the back den. This element was supposed to be an elegant way to delineate the living spaces from the dining areas, but as they grew older, had become a hazardous affectation.

22   Late at night I used to see infomercials for compression socks and back supports made with copper-infused fabric. Now they are advertising copper-infused face masks.

I order one, thinking, *nice pivot*.

There was a children's show I used to watch with my kids where the characters traveled by flying buffalo all over the earth's four kingdoms to learn the secrets of the elements so they could save the world. A teacher they encountered in one episode advised the young hero that he had to cleanse himself of all fear, guilt, disappointment, grief, lies, illusions, and attachments, if he was to become the master of his own inner power.

As my son and daughter imitated the fighting stances of the water village, the fire village, the earth village and the air village, I watched too, trying to release my flaws and fears, even though I knew they would last long after the final episode of the series.

The summer after my freshman year of college, I worked at an amusement park, arriving every day to change into my uniform of a long orange skirt and an orange and white striped blouse with short puffy sleeves. After tying a delicate black bow around my neck, I would stash my street clothes in a locker and enter the park through a back passageway that opened up near the main street of magic shops and ice cream parlors.

I had grown up going to the park and I thought I might

hate knowing what it was like behind the scenes, but I didn't. I loved knowing there was a secret basketball court under the snow-covered mountain, and that the asteroids in the space rollercoaster were really videos of highly magnified chocolate chip cookies.

Familiarity had only made me love it more.

My dog and I walk by the ocean, among the ruins, where she likes to roll in the salty grass and feel the soft sand underneath the pads of her feet. Once she discovered a giant duffel bag behind a tree and I felt culpable, like we had barged into somebody else's home.

On the way back through the parking lot, we passed a large hawk sitting on the roof rack of a Subaru. He was confident, his dark eyes unblinking, as if he fully expected someone to take him to his chosen destination.

23   But sometimes a man is just so so unattainable, how can you not want to keep him for yourself?

I mean, when something gets in, makes its way through all the hard surfaces, the built-up layers of sediment, the brambles and buttresses, the icy winds, the howling—that's really something, isn't it?

Because sometimes a violence grips me, absolutely grips me, and I want to rip up everything I have made—the clothes, the drawings, the recipe cards.

Us.

I still fall in love with inventing my own trouble.

When my daughter was a teenager, I asked her if she and her friends played hard to get with the boys at school.

She looked at me, squinted, and said, "You play stupid games, you win stupid prizes."

Robert Ripley sewed a fish and a monkey's bodies together and said it was a mermaid from the Fiji Islands. People believed it for years.

There might be those who believe it still.

24   Our house has been through several iterations. From earthquake shack to divided duplex, to built-on single family dwelling, decks added. We were here for the last stage.

It felt good to have a project; we were good together on it. The kids loved it too—climbing on the scaffolding, an illicit jungle gym where they could peer into their own bedroom windows.

That was years ago now; things are falling apart, as things do. The rotting wood of the patio, the patched-up leaks that were never repainted. How we both said, *We'll get to it after this, after that.* We did mean it; at least if felt as if we did.

But then time passed, and the patches receded in our minds, and therefore, in our lives.

That's how I know we are getting old. *Let someone else deal with that*, I think, looking at the ceiling.

As if I'm getting ready to leave; either this house, or this earth.

I don't know which, but it will be one or the other, it has to be.

25   The will, though, it remains. The way something catches your attention—a movement, even if it is just dust mote floating through a stray ray of light—and your eyes follow it, to see what is causing the change in your awareness.

It's the same now, though, as before the pandemic began. You have to decide what to spend your images on.

As in a clean mirror, my therapist would say.

And the collective consciousness—that too can become sick, infected with the viruses of people's emotions. You can see it in the streets, and especially online, where people hide behind fake identities to voice their true feelings.

Still, I keep thinking that there is hope. After all, Hitler wasn't elected—his *party* was elected, and they *appointed* him Chancellor. So more like a Prime Minister, and less like a President.

My husband thinks this is a silly distinction, but I cling to it. That Democracy is—that it can be—different.

How to use hate to inoculate myself to hate, that's what I want. To become stronger through controlled exposure, a vaccination, one that leaves a scar, to remind me of how things used to be.

26   No one can build something out of nothing, which means that there is no such thing as a self-made man.

Even the Dalai Lama had to be taught how to be the Dalai Lama. It took years of study; he started his training when he was four.

Emily Dickinson never married. Jane Austen never married. Louisa May Alcott never married. Harper Lee never married. Coco Chanel never married.

Nabokov married a brilliant woman, Vera, who wrote all his letters for him, taught his classes when he was sick, *and* pulled the pages of *Lolita* out of a bonfire when her husband tried to burn it.

Simone de Beauvoir never married.

Oprah Winfrey never married.

Ruth Bader Ginsburg and Martin Ginsburg met on a blind date. After they married, Martin did all the cooking and campaigned for Ruth's nomination to the Supreme Court.

Now *that* was a marriage.

The first time my husband and I went to Europe, he was not my husband yet. We went to a fancy restaurant on the banks of Lake Geneva and ordered the prix fixe meal because we couldn't read the menu. We felt very cosmopolitan.

The table, with its elegant cloth napkins and silver serving ware; the pristine lake where a fountain sprayed a jet of water like a giant sprinkler.

The first course came out and the waiter removed the silver cover with a flourish to show a plate of thin slices of raw meat.

It was carpaccio. A carpaccio made of horsemeat.

27　　On the day we scattered my father's ashes into the ocean, a seal swam around the pier where we stood looking at the waves. My mother, sister, and I first saw it, big, on one side of the pier, while I sprinkled my tablespoon of ash from one of my mother's empty pill bottles, along with a small shiny dime, into the water.

By the time we walked to the end of the pier and then around to the other side, the seal had moved too; we could just make out his tiny head bobbing up from the bright sunlight glinting on the blue waves.

Maybe he had returned to us in his selkie skin, so his spirit could linger in the Bardo of the ocean.

My mother liked the idea of Dad coming back to visit us as a seal. She believed in ghosts because her father came to her in her dreams whenever he wanted to tell her something important. Gung Gung had died when I was five and he was already ghost-like to me before he passed away—a small man with sharp cheekbones and keen, dark eyes.

We would sometimes visit him at his poultry store in Chinatown, where I had to walk past cages and cages filled with chickens and ducks as I made my way to his little office at the very back of the building.

The birds felt like ghosts to me, cooing in the dim light.

28   *We found you under a haystack,* our mother said whenever we asked her to tell us about when we were born. Daddy owned a dairy, so it was not impossible, but we assumed she was joking with us, her silly rabbits.

But then my sister and I found out that we were adopted, and we decided that we were actually mushrooms.

"Yeah, kept in the dark and covered with shit," my sister remarked.

Then the two of us laughed and laughed.

29   Knocking on different doors—white ones, blue ones, red ones, yellow ones—I kept trying to find new people in new places, but whenever the doors opened, my mother and father were standing there, yet again.

> The soil of survival is blocked by fear.
> The rain of pleasure is blocked by guilt.
> The magma of willpower is blocked by shame.
> The sky of the heart is blocked by grief.
> The ore of the self is blocked by delusion.
> The iris of intuition is blocked by disconnection.
> The orion of the mind is blocked by attachment.

> Our subtle body and its discontents.

> Like the Japanese, I wanted a phone to call the wind.

30   Depression turns one's life into a very pointless movie, one that can be described in a few moth-eaten words:

Man gets stuck on island, makes friends with volleyball.

Man runs a lot, meets a bunch of people, eats chocolate.

Man jumps into a river, is saved by old guy wearing a nightgown. Bells ring.

Man marches to ocean, makes salt.

Man loves his sled.

Bored wife dresses up, eats cake.

Governess falls for boss, finds his first wife in the attic, too late.

Bored politician's wife chats up local soldier.

Woman won't marry adopted brother, his revenge ruins family.

Bored housewife gets pixie cut, gives birth to the antichrist.

Big fish eats boat.

(Movie Key: *Castaway, Forrest Gump, It's a Wonderful Life, Gandhi, Citizen Kane, Marie Antoinette, Jane Eyre, Madame Bovary, Wuthering Heights, Rosemary's Baby, Moby Dick*.)

31   My husband drinks his whiskey with a splash of water, which he says makes the liquor taste more like itself.

I marvel at how this can be, that dilution can make something more itself, rather than something less than what it was.

Coming upon a luna moth in the doorway of my parent's home one hot Southern California night. It is summer and my children revel in the heat, the delight of not having to wear a jacket everywhere they go, even after the sun sets.

And the moth, pale green, the size of a dinner plate. Bigger than the moon in the sky, and just as luminous.

The individual segments that make up a blackberry fruit are called drupelet. Each drupelet bursts when you bite it, a tiny explosion of juice.

Explosion, or eruption? Here, I like explosion.

Elsewhere, I might change my mind.

It used to take the wax from 10,000 bees to make a celebrity's statue for Hollywood's Wax Museum. Now only the head of the statue is crafted of beeswax; the body is made of fiberglass.

And still the bees go on, doing the everyday work of saving the planet.

32   My husband and I drive up to the top of Twin Peaks to see the lights of the skyline, the flashing score on the Bay Bridge, the LED dancers leaping around the tip of the SalesForce Tower, and it is mesmerizing. From here it's hard to believe in light pollution, but above us there are constellations, so many stars we cannot see.

The first time we made love, it was in the forest. We had gone backpacking, and the trees were tall, but did not obscure the night sky. We felt natural, our animal selves.

Some things need the darkness to grow.

Though words still slipped into the black hole of my throat, never to be seen again.

When I looked into the sky, the missing words didn't matter.

When I looked into people's faces—boxes of a crossword puzzle—it did.

First layer, terror—second layer, doubt—third layer, dread—fourth layer, worry—fifth layer, panic—sixth layer, helplessness—seventh layer, guilt—eighth layer, depression.

Which leads to insomnia.

There are signs all over the beach warning against sneaker waves, rogue waves, rip waves that come out of nowhere and will snatch you off the sand.

Because it is impossible to call out for help when you are choking on your heart.

33   I used to collect wind-up toys well into adulthood. A rabbit that skipped rope, a frog that did backflips, a tiger that rolled over like a kitten.

A pair of chattering teeth.

Soft socks are such a small thing, but surprisingly important.

For a few years, my children too collected little charms from the vending machines on Clement Street. Small figures of Winnie the Pooh dressed up as different things.

At first, the toys were delightful—Winnie the Pooh dressed like a bumblebee, Winnie the Pooh dressed like a daisy.

As time went on, Pooh morphed into other animals as well—Winnie the Pooh as a lion, Winnie the Pooh as a penguin, a panda bear.

Then, even stranger iterations—Winnie the Pooh as a pineapple, Winnie the Pooh as a starfish. Winnie the Pooh as a spiral bound notebook. A pencil. A tube of paint.

A flamingo.

When the kids got a duplicate Pooh, which was often, they traded with their friends to increase the circulation of Poohs. I wondered how many different designs the makers of these Pooh Bears were required to create—and what they were smoking when they were doing it.

34   I was still trying to enter the gateless gate, though when I typed the words, autocorrect changed the phrase to the *dateless date*.

This is what I will write on my Tinder profile, if I ever have one.

"Willing to go on a *dateless date*."

35   I can hear leaf blowers all over our neighborhood.
      Occasionally, I use one myself.
      And the Tuesday noon siren that used to signal a city-wide
practice alarm.
      Are we still practicing? I wonder when I hear it now.

      Sometimes I hear children playing in someone's backyard
nearby, but I can't see them. Their voices are like those from an old
television show, *The Brady Bunch*, or perhaps *The Twilight Zone*.

      I smile at the clerks at the grocery store from behind my mask
and I hope they can feel it, even if they can't see me doing it.

      Our dog barks at so many things in the backyard: skunks,
opossums, blue jays, raccoons.
      The raccoons are especially brazen, coming through the dog
door at night to drink from her water dish. Sometimes they sit on the
fence and tease her.
      We have fingers, you don't.

      Once I found a shiny blue ladybug walking along our blue
cactus planter. I thought it might be a mutant, but no, blue ladybugs
are a thing, native to Australia.
      How this one came to my backyard in America is a mystery.
      After that day, I never saw her again, but I still look for her, a
blessing.

36   After the DNA test results came back and revealed that my sister and I *were* siblings, but that *we weren't* biologically related to our parents, I read all the online adoption articles I could find. They had headlines like "When Your Father Is Not Your Father: DNA tests can reveal more than you bargained for." And, "How a DNA Testing Kit Revealed a Family Secret Hidden for 54 Years."

"Well at least yours is an adoption story," my husband said when I described these articles to him. "And not 'Home DNA Results Linked to Cold Case Murder.'"

I love my husband, but I am the kind of person who will run across the intersection if the pedestrian light is still flashing; my husband will wait if there are ten seconds or less counting down.

This means we have spent a significant portion of our marriage standing on opposite sides of the street—me, waiting impatiently for him, him waiting for the light to change again, tolerating my impatience.

37   When my mother visited San Francisco to see her grandchildren, she objected to the naked people who walked around the Castro. Most of these people were men, but there was the occasional woman too. They tended to hang out at the parklet by the cable car turnaround.

"What about your kids?" she demanded as we drove through the neighborhood with the kids in the backseat. "What about their rights to not see nude old men on the streets?"

I spoke over my shoulder to them. "Should I drive a different route to school?" I asked my children.

"Why?" my son asked, not looking up from his Gameboy.

"To avoid the naked dudes," I answered.

"What naked dudes?" he asked, still not looking up.

The newly installed crosswalks, rainbow colored, however, received my mother's approval.

After a slow start, the proliferation of masks for sale was swift. There were everyday, casual masks, dressy masks, sporty masks for exercising, dainty masks, and psychedelic masks that were once the domain of music festivals.

I bought my mother a mask with black sequins and made her a necklace of faux pearls so she could wear it around her neck.

38   When did we stop worrying about falling into quicksand? When my sister and I were kids, it always seemed like we were on the verge of being swallowed up by the ground.

Oh yes, I remember now—the quicksand was replaced by sharks.

And I know exactly the day it happened: June 20, 1975. The opening day of the movie *Jaws*.

Now we have *Shark Week, When Sharks Attack, Sharks Vs. Dolphins*, and *Megashark*. Also, *Sharknado 1-6, DinoShark, Avalanche Sharks*, and *Ghost Shark, Two-Headed Shark Attack, Three-Headed Shark Attack, Four-Headed Shark Attack, Five-Headed Shark Attack*, and *Six-Headed Shark Attack*.

Seven-Headed Shark Attack is set for release in 2029.

According to the survival guides, if you encounter a shark, you are supposed to poke it in the eye.

If you run into a mountain lion, you are supposed to act as if you are bigger than you really are.

Which is hard for some people, having been told to make themselves small for their entire lives.

One grows vigilant when raised by an unpredictable animal.

39   As girls, we learned through diffusion. We *absorbed* lessons.

And when we went into the water, we learned through osmosis.

Knowledge comes in through the skin, a permeable membrane.

I made all the obvious mistakes.

When my daughter was born, the doctor said he wanted to talk to me, privately. "Is there anything you want to tell me?" he asked raising his eyebrows. "About what?" I asked in return, thinking it must be something embarrassing. "About those," he said, tipping his head to the scratches, which were all over my back. In a moment of surprise, I realized he wanted to know if my husband hurt me. "No," I told him truthfully. "I did that myself."

I was surprised the scratches were that bad since I hadn't been able to see them.

"Oh," the doctor replied, and that was that.

Later, I wondered whether it was part of a doctor's training, to look for signs of abuse, and I thought even if it wasn't, it was nice that my doctor had asked.

When I told my husband what had happened, he said, "You really need to get help for your eczema."

All my life my mother always said I was too sensitive; now it seemed as though my emotions were coming out through my skin.

An eruption.

40   In the late afternoon, the wind outside our window blows relentlessly, an ocean of swirling air.

The 4pm fog spills over the hill and into our little valley, a microclimate of mist.

Our house is the ship that sails through these currents, navigates the mist, and rocks us to sleep.

An hour and a half south of our home, there is a redwood forest in the middle of an ancient ocean bed. When you hike there, sometimes the trail is covered in layers of needles and leaves when suddenly you will be slogging through a small dune of finely milled sand, even though you are miles and miles from the sea.

I used to eat an avocado every day, on toast, on ramen, or all by itself, scooping out the fruit's smooth green flesh with a spoon, like ice cream.

It sent my cholesterol through the roof, but I couldn't stop. All those fatty oils clogging up my veins sliding me toward some horizon, some self-made oblivion.

Once, an acupuncturist took my wrist in his hand to feel my pulse. He told me to stick out my tongue and looked at it as if he was examining a sea creature—a seal, perhaps—who had eaten too many mercury-filled fish.

When I die, I've told my husband that I want to be buried in a compostable coffin, wearing a mushroom-infused shroud.

So in death I will to continue to *grow*.

41   After our son was born, only my husband could sleep at night. I stayed up with the baby, rocking, rocking, rocking, repeating the same lullaby to him for hours. *Hey everybody have you heard, I'm gonna buy you a mockingbird. And if that bird don't sing, I'm gonna buy you a diamond ring.*

After I ran out of the regular verses, I made up more. *And if that bear don't poop in the woods, I'm gonna forage in the field for more food. And that's why, I keep telling everybody, say, yeah, yeah, yeah, yeah, yeah.*

I wasn't even sure I should have kids because I was a terrible gardener. I was the kind of person who threw seeds at the ground, watered haphazardly, and hoped for the best.

What if I did that with children?

My husband and I waited until we had been married ten years before we had our first baby. Perhaps that was a sign. Either we were extra ready, or we weren't ready at all.

And five years later, we had our daughter. It was like we had waited so long to become parents, and then we tried to stretch it out as long as we could.

42   When she was a baby, my daughter's eyes were large and round, her head even larger and rounder. I would go into her room at night to find her sitting up in her crib, eyes staring at me, unblinking. It was unnerving to be unnerved by your own child, to come upon her silent stare in the pitch black of the night.

I became obsessed with efficiency, buying labor-saving devices, and things to save time, because time seemed extra important. An instant cooking pot, wool dryer balls, a robot to vacuum the floors, another to clean the roof gutters. Sock and underwear organizers. I bought a container with special slots for wrapping paper and rolls of ribbon. Telescoping dusters. Wooden knife blocks and plastic cereal holders. A pot to store the garden hose, coiled like a snake.

People said I was *nesting*.

But I was trying to fend off *disaster*.

On a normal day, I could be awkward and self-conscious, riven with anxiety.

But if there was an emergency, everyone would agree that I was your man.

43 Under the sky, among the trees, I was genderless. Not a woman or a man, I felt most like myself in their arboreal company.

As in a library, in the company of books.

Leaves of grass.

Was I the wave, or the rider who missed the wave?

The history of the world, made up of so much water.

What we call orca whales are really the largest dolphins on earth.

A writing prompt: Go outside and listen quietly for ten minutes. Write a poem to the sounds you hear, and one to the sounds you cannot not hear.

44 I like how Australians refer to their nation as "The Lucky Country," even though they are home to the box jellyfish, the bull shark, the taipan snake, the saltwater crocodile. The cassowary, the blue-ringed octopus, the red-backed spider.

So many things that could kill you.

At the amusement park where I worked during the summers, the punchline on the boat ride through the jungle was this: "And now for the most dangerous part of your journey: Coming back to the Southern California freeways."

That made the passengers laugh, because it was true.

45   Before the pandemic, I liked taking public transportation. Riding the streetcars, a red blood cell moving along the arteries of the city, seeing so much I might have missed.

The house with the jungle scene painted on the front. The view of the downtown skyline from the palm-treed park. Tracks wound through people's backyards in the hills, passing a Spanish-tiled house with a giant pipe organ in the window. Lush bougainvillea spouted fountains of magenta petals. Groups of kids carrying backpacks on their way to or from the high school next to the old mission, the oldest surviving building in the city.

As long as I wasn't in a hurry, all of this was mine, the entire city and its contents. My fellow riders reading the city's pages along with me.

Now I have to calculate the time of day, how closely packed the streetcars will be, and how long the trip will take.

Is it worth it to be out in the world?

The health department has drawn white chalk circles on the grass, so we can safely sit at the park.

In addition to my therapist, I see my regular doctor on Zoom now as well.

"We discourage people from smoking marijuana, because COVID-19 attacks the lungs," he told me at my pandemic appointment. He said he wanted to check in with his patients just in case they didn't want to come to the hospital anymore.

"Oh dear," I murmured, having just bought a packet of blunts at my neighborhood dispensary.

"That's why," my doctor continued, "we tell all our patients that edibles are the way to go."

Logging off the call, I had the feeling that this was possibly the most *San Francisco conversation* I'd ever had.

46 My therapist thinks my disjunction started when I was molested as a child. I had not thought about it in years, but when my daughter turned six, I suddenly remembered, and though I tried, I couldn't forget it again, not the way I had when I was a child. I begged my therapist to tell me how I could move on; that I knew there wasn't anything I could do about it, so why was I so wracked about it now?

"Do you know the myth of Persephone?" my therapist asked.

I did. Persephone, kidnapped and raped by her uncle Hades and held against her will in the Underworld.

"But remember, her mother Demeter searched for her, refused to let the earth bear fruit until Persephone was returned to her," my therapist said. "At least for a part of each year."

Ah yes, I said. I knew the story.

"Imagine Persephone trapped in the Underworld, without Demeter to help her return to the Upperworld," said my therapist.

"That would be terrible," I blurted out, thinking of my own children, how frightened they would be, how desperate I would be to find them. How any mother would feel that way, if she knew. "To be left there all by yourself."

"It was terrible," my therapist said gently. "That you were left there by yourself."

47　　"You hold memories in your body, not just your mind," my therapist also says.

I wish my body held different memories, but don't we all?

My husband's body holds different memories, and that's good. It's why we can be together. Our bodies fit together because our memories do not.

The smoothness of his skin is a promise that everything will be all right, the lightness of his touch will make their own memories on my body, different from the ones I grew up with.

At first, I was worried that my husband wouldn't want me to have the memories that I had. Then what would I do?

And that took trust too.

On the yoga mat, my body's memories, its stories, come flying out. The tightness around my chest, around my eyes—that old fear, that old sadness.

Let it go, whispers the pose, both in the doing and in the undoing. Muscles, as springboard, as catapult.

You can only hold your breath for so long.

48 In high school, my sophomore English teacher assigned a book titled *The Hidden Persuaders* by a man named Vance Packard. I think she hoped we would have discussions about scotch companies selling alcohol by airbrushing images of naked women into the ice cubes, about how corporations were commandeering our minds for consumerist ends.

Instead, we laughed at her behind her back because she dyed her hair blond to look younger, because she came to class in leopard print blouses and skirts that were much too short. Her knees were little Parker rolls of fat, exposed to our critical gaze.

So we failed our first lesson—to focus on the message, not the messenger.

A journalism professor in college, on the other hand, assigned my class a book called *Megatrends*, which taught us how to manipulate people by creating artificial in-groups and aspirational desires.

It was like being taught to be the bully instead of the bullied.

49   Like Penelope, I can knit and unknit the same shawl over and over, as many times as I like.

I decide when to continue.

I decide when it's done.

My dog has her own stink and she doesn't care what anyone thinks about it.

But all dogs have the same bacteria that makes their paws smell like corn chips.

We have a cherry tree in the backyard that bears no fruit. Every March the tree is filled with pink blooms that blow away on the first windy day of Spring, covering the ground with petals that look like snow.

I wish I could cry, because people like you better if they know you are sad. If you look all right to them, then you must be ok.

Perhaps my tear ducts are also depressed.

"No one is going to feel sorry for me," a famous chef once said on his television show when asked why he rarely talked about his persistent feelings of depression. "I'm famous, I've got a great job, I've got good friends—what do I have to be depressed about? No one wants to be *that* guy." Which I took to mean a whiner, an ingrate, a wimp.

50   "Why are you laughing?" my therapist once asked as I described the time I cut myself on a piece of broken glass and fainted, only to find my mother standing over my prone body yelling, *Get up! You're scaring me!*

I stopped for a moment, though I could tell my face was still smiling. "Because if it isn't funny, then what is it?" I said, puzzled.

The giraffe, though nonsensical, has everything she needs to exist, including the largest heart of all land-dwelling mammals. To have a heart that big, and a valve in your neck so you don't pass out every time you lean over for a drink of water, miraculous.

51   The best job I ever had was being a publisher's rep because I worked from home, not in an office. I had a company car, a silver Chevy Caprice that I nicknamed "The Random-Mobile."

I drove long distances in the Random-Mobile visiting little bookstores, where the buyers were so surprised to see an actual person that they gave me overly large orders, mostly mystery books and romance novels.

Sometimes I'd spend the whole day counting inventories and filling out forms and I would come home feeling like a child let loose in a library to play among the stacks.

One of my favorite books starts, "You are about to begin reading Italo Calvino's new novel, *If on a winter's night a traveler.* Relax."

The text goes on to narrate you into the book as you read it. "Adjust the light so you won't strain your eyes. What are you waiting for?" And, "Let's see how it begins."

All stories transport you somewhere, but this one includes you in the telling.

Is it wrong to want someone, somewhere, to hold you, if only in their minds?

How do you put yourself into your own heart?

In other words, if you have to fake it until you make it, what happens if you never make it?

52   When my children were growing up, I had a rule that we do one active thing each day. One day was for swimming lessons, another day we went to a playground in a different neighborhood of the city. There were art days, music days, and later, karate days and clarinet days. There were volleyball days, soccer days, and once in a while, day off days.

And in this way, I knew I still had to live.

At the parks, though, women with their children often mistook me for my children's nanny.

"Oh," they would say, flustered, when I said I was *the mother,* "They must take after their father. Is he Caucasian?"

"Caucasian is almost Asian," my sister said when I told her of these encounters. "We're Asian. He's Ca-Ca Asian."

So people think I'm the nanny. And guess that my children are Portuguese.

Ambiguously ethnic, as my daughter puts it.

I spritz the lavender eau de toilette on my pillow at night, trying to tell the receptors in my brain to do what Italo Calvino told me to do when I opened his novel: *Relax.*

53   There are yoga poses I love doing—Trikonasana (triangle pose), Urdhva Mukha Svanasana (upward facing dog pose), Salamba Sarvangasana (shoulder stand)—and the poses I love once I'm *finished* doing them—Dhanurasana (bow pose), Virabhadrasana III (Warrior 3 pose), Adho Mukha Vrksasana (handstand).

And in that way, I love them all.

The *doing* of some, and the *releasing* of others.

54   On Thanksgiving, I always cook a turkey so we can make jook—Chinese rice porridge—with the leftovers the next day. This is how we celebrate being American and Chinese: one bowl at a time.

Then my daughter took it to the next level by putting her jook into a tortilla shell. When I asked why, she replied, "Because everything tastes better in a taco."

55   When I logged on to online adoption discussions, many of the comments went along these lines:

Your biological parents gave you up so you would have a better life.

You're lucky you grew up in the US and not in China.
You know they drown unwanted baby girls in China.
Your adopted parents are your real parents.
You should be happy.
You should be grateful.
Your adoptive parents love you.
Your birth parents love you.
You shouldn't be so needy.

(Translation Key: *You're lucky, lucky, lucky, be happy, happy, happy, be grateful, grateful, grateful.*)

They were the same conversations I read about immigration. You're lucky! Forget where you came from. Don't think about that. Don't act like them anymore, don't talk like them, don't eat like them.

You're living in our country now.
We're your family.
Be like us.

"I was a Tiger Mother before there was a name for it," my mother loves to tell people. It's her love language, written in a tongue I longed to translate.

Because it was love that drove all of us to do what we did,
when it should have been the thing that set us free.

My parents taught me everything I knew about love and my
children taught me everything I didn't know about love.

The tenderness I have for all of them could fill an ocean.

There is a bridge in China named "The Lucky Knot."
In the shape of a Möbius strip, it has no beginning and no end.
Pedestrians can cross by passing through five round moon gates along
the platform's infinite loop, which rises high over the Dragon King
Harbor River.

56   Eighty percent of a person's neural pathways go from the body to the brain. Only twenty percent go from the brain back to the body.

If a person gets stuck in fight or flight mode, it can imitate a normal state of being.

The world is not a mutually exclusive ecosystem.
That is why we have the platypus.
And high-functioning depression.

Which can lead to selective mutism.

Question: What if the way you love is backwards?
Answer: Turn your love inside out.

57   When my husband and I had children, it would have been easier in some ways to move closer to family. But in other ways, it would have been harder, so we stayed where we were, far away.

It was an old story, and this version was ours.

I was very good at giving people what they wanted, especially if they looked me in the eye when they asked.

Like sea creatures, we emit electrical impulses to those around us: Here is my location, this is my size and shape, these are my wounds.

A shark can sense an injured fish from a mile away. It isn't the blood they're after, it's the vibration.

58   At a writing conference, a medium-famous male writer invited me to hang out with a group of the faculty, which included his friend, a very famous male poet. When I arrived at the restaurant at the appointed time, I found the medium-famous male writer alone at the bar.

"Sorry it's just me," he said, "Everyone else flaked out."

Five minutes into the conversation, he just happened to mention that he dated a medium-famous female Asian American comedian, whom he would drive to various orgies in LA.

In my head I was shouting, *Fuck this.* But just in my head.

Was my work like a bee pollinating flowers? Necessary, but unremunerated?

Plus, all of the *emotional* labor, also unpaid.

A phase is something you go through on your way to becoming something else. A trait is something you are, something that exudes from you wherever you go.

I kept expecting to outgrow my credulity, but instead it was something I kept opening, a knocked door.

"You don't always have to open the door just because someone knocks." From my therapist.

"I don't?"

"And sometimes you can do the knocking."

"I can?"

When my children were small, they would play a car game called "Sweet and Sour." As we drove through the city, they would wave at the other drivers whenever we came to a red light or a stop sign. If the driver waved back, they got a "sweet."

If the driver ignored them, that was a "sour."

59   "You believe in the Golden Rule," my sister says. "That's your problem."

"What can I say?" I ask. "I'm an optimist."

"No," she answers. "You're a disaster."

I am a disaster, but I try to keep it to myself. That's something, isn't it?

"It's like you took a vow, or something," my best friend tells me. We've known each other even longer than either of us has been married, so we can talk. "Like the Hippocratic oath."

"Is that bad?" I ask.

"Well, you're not a doctor, for one thing."

And still, I persisted, is what I would say.

60   So much effort goes into creating and storing energy. The entire point of the engine room on an aircraft carrier is to boil water. Steam is what moves the massive ship.

We are the product of sunlight.

Our cars are fossil slaves, part of our chemical signature.

61   Procrastinating induces a feeling of terror, which is the most reliable way for me to get things done.

It really doesn't matter which way you install the toilet paper, so why does it feel *so wrong* when the end hangs under the roll instead of over it?

One of the things I admire most about animals: *They do not mourn what they never had.*

62   An imaginary conversation with Barbara Walters:
     BW: If you were a tree, what kind of tree would you be?
     Me: A quaking aspen.
     BW: Why?
     Me: I want to turn my shaking into beauty.

     I sometimes find myself wondering, which pine tree has bark
that smells of vanilla, Ponderosa, or Lodgepole?

63   In every grove of trees, there is a mother tree who spaces out the new saplings so they receive the most light and water. The mother tree sends sugars through her roots to the growing grove, communicates with the others via silky fungi filaments that run through the earth from her roots to theirs.

Many people know that Van Gogh only sold one painting during his lifetime, even though his brother Theo was an art dealer.

Theo died six months after Vincent, leaving Theo's wife, Johanna, alone with a young son, all of his brother's paintings and nothing else.

They had only been married for two years.

Johanna, who had been an English teacher before marrying, took Theo's and Vincent's letters and began editing them and putting them into order while making money by translating French and English stories into Dutch.

She also took the 200 paintings Vincent had left to Theo and that Theo had left to her, and she made them famous.

So thank you, Johanna Van Gogh, for *Starry Night* and *Sunflowers*, *Irises* and *Cypress Trees, Wheatfield with Crows, Self-Portrait with Bandana*, and *The Sower*.

64   Sometimes when I get into bed, my husband smells like buttered popcorn.

Mmm, good pheromones.

Like a crow, I collect shiny things.

Beads, yarn, pictures, words.

Then I make my treasures into something else: a necklace, a sweater, a tapestry, a poem.

Life as collage—what we choose and what we make of what we choose.

65   Our son was born first; our daughter five years later. So for the first five years of his life, my son was an only child. And then, when he left home for college, my daughter became an only child until she graduated from high school.

So I knew my son best as a small child, but I knew my daughter best as a young adult.

> I imagine biographies of ancient women like this:
> *Helen of Troy: Sex and the Spartan Girl.*
> *Medea: A Bad Divorce.*
> *Penelope: The Long Goodbye.*
> *Demeter: Mother of the Year.*

66   When museums were closed during the pandemic, I was bereft. I went to museums the way some people go to church, for the solace, and the beauty. I was worried about people gathering indoors, of course, but I understood why they didn't want to give it up, their Sunday ritual.

If a church was the only place I could meet my soul, I might risk the virus and go there too.

To see the gold brushed garments of Klimt's *The Kiss*, to feel the rapture of that embrace.

To hope to capture the ineffable.

67   Like Proust, Edith Wharton wrote her books while lying in bed.

As did Mark Twain.

And Truman Capote.

Not only did William Wordsworth write in bed, he also kept the room completely dark, often losing his pages in the gloom.

Ernest Hemingway, however, wrote standing up.

There is another author who could only write while he was walking, but I've forgotten his name.

A writing prompt: Write a poem while you are walking. Can you feel the rhythm of the words creating a path on the page?

68 It takes a sloth all day to climb down from his branch to poop. And another day to climb back up. That's two whole days just to go to the bathroom.

And he doesn't give a damn what you think about it.

The jellyfish has no brain at all, and yet thrives in the open ocean, adapting to everything, even global warming.

I don't do drugs; I am *drugs*, said Salvador Dali.

A writing prompt: Write an iceberg, twice. The first time, show only the tip, the second time, the whole iceberg.

69 After his stroke, my father had to sit in a wheelchair because the left side of his body was paralyzed. My mother brought him home from the hospital because she said he wouldn't like being surrounded by strangers.

My father's face was unlined, his hair less gray than mine. We all marveled at this since he had spent his entire life working outdoors, mostly under an unrelenting sun.

"How do you know Dad wants to be home?" my sister asked. "He can't tell you."

"I know," our mother answered. She turned on some music, played my father's favorite singer, Dolly Parton.

As Dolly trilled about her coat of many colors, my father began to tap his right foot in time to the music. He didn't stop tapping until the song was finished.

Memory is a cairn, something that marks our paths. You set off fresh in the morning, on a trail headed for new vistas, but when you see that group of rocks, stacked in such a specific way, you suddenly realize, *oh, I've been here before.*

70   *You'll never know what I've done for you,* my mother would say, whenever I balked at doing my chores, whether it was washing the dishes or polishing the kitchen cabinets or scrubbing the bathroom sinks and tub.

And that's how I came to know that everything had to be earned, even love.

My parents vowed to keep our adoption a secret, telling each other there were good reasons to withhold it from us.

People can be so cruel, they said. *It's better if nobody knows, not even the children themselves.*

But then the internet came along.

Of the music of chance, there are many kinds.

71   Botanists thought that the dawn redwood had gone extinct, but then it was rediscovered on the other side of the world, in China.

Perhaps a person can be thought to be gone too, and then rediscovered in a remote and unlikely place.

Nobody—not even the people who study these things—knows why redwood trees grow so tall. Looking up, you would think they'd have immense roots dug deep into the ground, but they don't. A redwood's roots are very shallow, and they spread out and intertwine with the roots of other trees in their grove. That is how they live, grasping on to one another, holding each other up.

There is an albino version of the redwood, aka the ghost redwood. Its leaves are a silvery white, and do not make food from sunshine, like other plants do. Instead, they snuggle next to another redwood, a coast redwood, and share the sugars from its roots, gaining nourishment from its neighbor, its leaves almost invisible to those passing by.

72   You can only be seen, my therapist keeps reminding me, if you share yourself with other people.

When our mother finally gave us my sister's adoption report, we realized that she had planned for us to find them after she had died. That way she could tell herself that she wasn't really keeping our adoption a secret from us.

But she wouldn't actually have to tell us, either.

"See, I saved them," Mom said, handing the sheaf of papers to my sister.

If we had found the document after Mom was gone, it's possible we would have just thrown them away, not understanding what they were telling us or how important they were.

The adoption papers contained the basic facts: our biological mother was the oldest of seven children, our biological father was the oldest of six, and both their families were Chinese who had immigrated to Thailand in the 1930s. They met as college students and because of their shared background, they gravitated toward one another on the UCLA campus. Lonely, and so far from their homeland, they became a couple, so they could miss it together.

When our parents discovered they were going to have a baby, they decided they were too young, that it would be too hard to raise a child and go to school and that neither of them wanted to cut short their education and go home to their families back in Thailand.

Two and a half years later, our mother became pregnant with me.

When I asked my mother for my adoption records, she said that she didn't have them. "By the time you came along, we were too busy with the farm to ask for them."

73   Three hundred people live on the Italian volcano of Stromboli, mostly in the northeast corner of the island. A regular cascade of lava and rocks roll harmlessly down the western and eastern black slopes into the ocean. The fish can dart away from these debris, but crabs and lobsters are often not fast enough to get out of the way, and, unlike the local octopuses, cannot hear the low frequency sounds that precede an eruption.

Only three animals can hear the deep frequencies before a volcano erupts or an earthquake hits: whales, elephants, and octopuses. It would be impractical to have a domesticated whale or an elephant, but I think I would like to have an octopus to keep me company and to warn of the Big One that is due to hit San Francisco any day now.

On my walks, I sometimes pass the fire hydrant that saved San Francisco after the 1906 earthquake. It sits at the bottom of a small hill on the corner of Church and 20th Street by Dolores Park. It looks like any other fire hydrant, but an anonymous citizen keeps painting it gold.

74   I am very good at co-regulating, though that doesn't mean I'm nice.

And by co-regulating, I mean that my heartbeat will match your heartbeat, my breathing will synchronize with your breathing, my dendrites will entwine with your dendrites.

As if I'm only capable of *reflecting.*

So I understand why it's tempting to live in an echo chamber. It's too hard to keep attuning to other people—to have your thoughts get so tangled that you can't tell if you're thinking your own thoughts or those of the person you're with.

If I disagree with someone, it feels like my disagreement exists only relative to the other person's argument. Then is my disagreement even mine—or is it something I have made up just so I can have the feeling of *I am?*

When what I am really doing is connecting to you in a negative space?

How the Buddhists put it: *What did your face look like before your parents were born?*

A poem in search of a form.

A small sea monster lives in our brains, the hippocampus, and it swims through our memories.

75   For the first two weeks after we adopted our dog, she was completely silent; she did not make any sounds at all. Then some friends came over for dinner one night and she suddenly found her voice and wouldn't stop barking.

We tried to get her to stop her ruckus by commanding her, then by giving her treats. Finally, I sat on the ground and whispered into her ear until she quieted down, but every time one of our friends got up and moved to a different part of the house—from the kitchen to the dining room, or to the bathroom and back—our dog started barking again. As though people became strangers to her whenever they appeared somewhere else, suspect again.

This went on until we found a young woman who would take our dog for walks with a group of six or seven other dogs in parks all over the city. After a couple of months, our dog stopped barking at strangers, and when I remarked on this to the young woman one day, she replied, "It's because she's learned."

"Learned what?" I asked.

"That she can be safe in a crowd."

76   I have begun to tell my old sadness to come in, have a seat and a cup of tea. Then I go about my day, my companion sitting quietly at the table of my heart.

When my sadness has finished drinking her tea, I say she can leave whenever she wants to.

The door is right there, I say.

The opposite of an exorcism, inviting all the demons in.

Offering them something warm to drink.

We don't fault the sun for its fire, do we?

And if you have a beautiful verb, you can use it.

Trumpeting, for example.

Or *Leafing*.

A writing prompt: Write a poem about the thing you cannot say. If you still can't say it, write a poem about not being able to write about the thing you cannot say.

Here are some things my therapist has said to me:
        Talk to yourself in second person. It's ok.
        Act as if people like you and they will like you.
        Only love will beget love.
        Work only begets more work.
        Value values, not feelings.
        Fuck feelings.
        Value values, not achievements.
        But what if you were taught to value achievements? I ask.
        Then fuck that, says my therapist.

        Question: Why do you love your therapist?
        Answer: Because she makes me laugh.

78   After Mom gave us my sister's adoption papers, I was able to find a picture of our biological parents in an online yearbook from UCLA, circa 1958. Since there were only eight men and four women in the Thai Student Association, it was easy to winnow down the choices from there.

Through the website that tested our DNA, we were able to connect with a biological cousin. The cousin contacted her mother, our aunt, who told us that our mother had died young, of liver cancer. And that our mother had never married, never had any other children, as far as she knew.

Our aunt also said that our mother was smart, that she had worked for UNICEF in Chiang Mai, that she liked to buy her young nieces and nephews ice cream when they came to visit. The cousin didn't know what happened to our father, or why he and our mother hadn't gotten married after they graduated.

My sister and I have kept in touch with our birth cousin, who has two girls near the same age as my son and daughter. We wish each other Happy Birthday and Merry Christmas on Facebook, check in from time to time to share what our kids are up to.

Like me, she knits.

My sister and I talk about going to Thailand someday, to visit that alternative universe where we might have lived another life. I imagine the modern buzz of Bangkok, the lush green of the countryside, in such contrast to the small town where my father had his dairy.

We also talk about our bio father and whether we should try to contact him, to let him know we're here. That we're all grown up and still together. According the the Bruin yearbook, he was a business major, but no trace of any jobs he might have had appear when I google his name. He has no digital footprint in the States, no offspring who immigrated to America, no siblings or other relatives either.

We wonder if we have half-siblings, and what they would say if they knew about us. Maybe they do know about us.

Until we get to Thailand, we'll have to make do with what we can imagine.

"All this time I felt like a burden to our parents," I said to my sister, "Like I had to be perfect to make up for something that had happened, even though I couldn't figure out what that was."

"We weren't a burden," my sister responded, sensibly. "The secret was the burden—and it isn't ours to carry."

79   It is said that if you enter a labyrinth with a question in mind, the answer will come to you by the time you reach the end of the maze.

A writing prompt: Take a poem and start erasing words until you can see the bones of a new poem emerge.

All that we see or seem is but a dream within a dream, wrote Edgar Allan Poe.

And still, we keep running up that hill. Running up that hill with the raven-haired singer's hounds of love.

#####

Acknowledgements

This book was written in the isolation of the pandemic, but over the years I have been blessed by friends and writers who have helped keep my writing going in crucial ways. Thank you all, especially to Lisa K. Buchanan, whose enthusiastic reading and joyful conversation I will always cherish.

I'm grateful to Kundiman, the Provincetown Fine Arts Workshop, and the Vermont Studio Center for their encouragement and support.

Special thanks to Matthew Salesses for choosing Bridge Of Knots for the fiction award. I'm honored by your belief in my work.

The care Gold Line Press put into my manuscript and the pleasure of the process will always be with me. Many thanks to Krishna Narayanamurti, Sam Cohen, Sara Fetherolf, and Thomas Renjilian, and also to Sandra Rosales, for the beautiful cover design.

To Peter, Allie and Gigi, and my family, all my love and thanks.

C.E. Shue holds an MFA from the University of San Francisco and has been published in *Drunken Boat, Entropy, Washington Square, Sparkle & Blink, Flash Fiction Review, Paragraph, E*Ratio, Spiral Orb, Lumina, Storyscape, The Satirist, flock, Poet As Radio, Switchback, The Collagist*, and other journals. The recipient of scholarships and grants from USF, The Provincetown Fine Arts Workshop, Vermont Studio Center, and Kundiman, she was a longtime board member for The Bay Area Generations reading series. You can contact her via her website: www.invisibleadventure.com